Lonnie, The Lobster Knight

and a Seahorse from the Isle of Wight

Written by: **Angela Frank**

Illustrated by : George Koftis

Author: Angela Frank
Adapted in to English: Filitsa Mullen

twitter- https://twitter.com/gelafrank

Illustrations: George Koftis

E-mail:gelafrank@hotmail.com
Angel's art publishing
E-shop: http://www.aggelikipapadopoulou-e-shop.com/

Book Design: Fylatos
ISBN 978-960-9691-10-9

Lonnie, the Lobster Knight
And a Seahorse from the Isle of Wight

Angela Frank

ILLUSTRATIONS George Koftis

Dedicated to Zoe and Chris

In the blue waters around the island of Rhodes there is a rocky house where **Lonnie** the Lobster lives with his family.

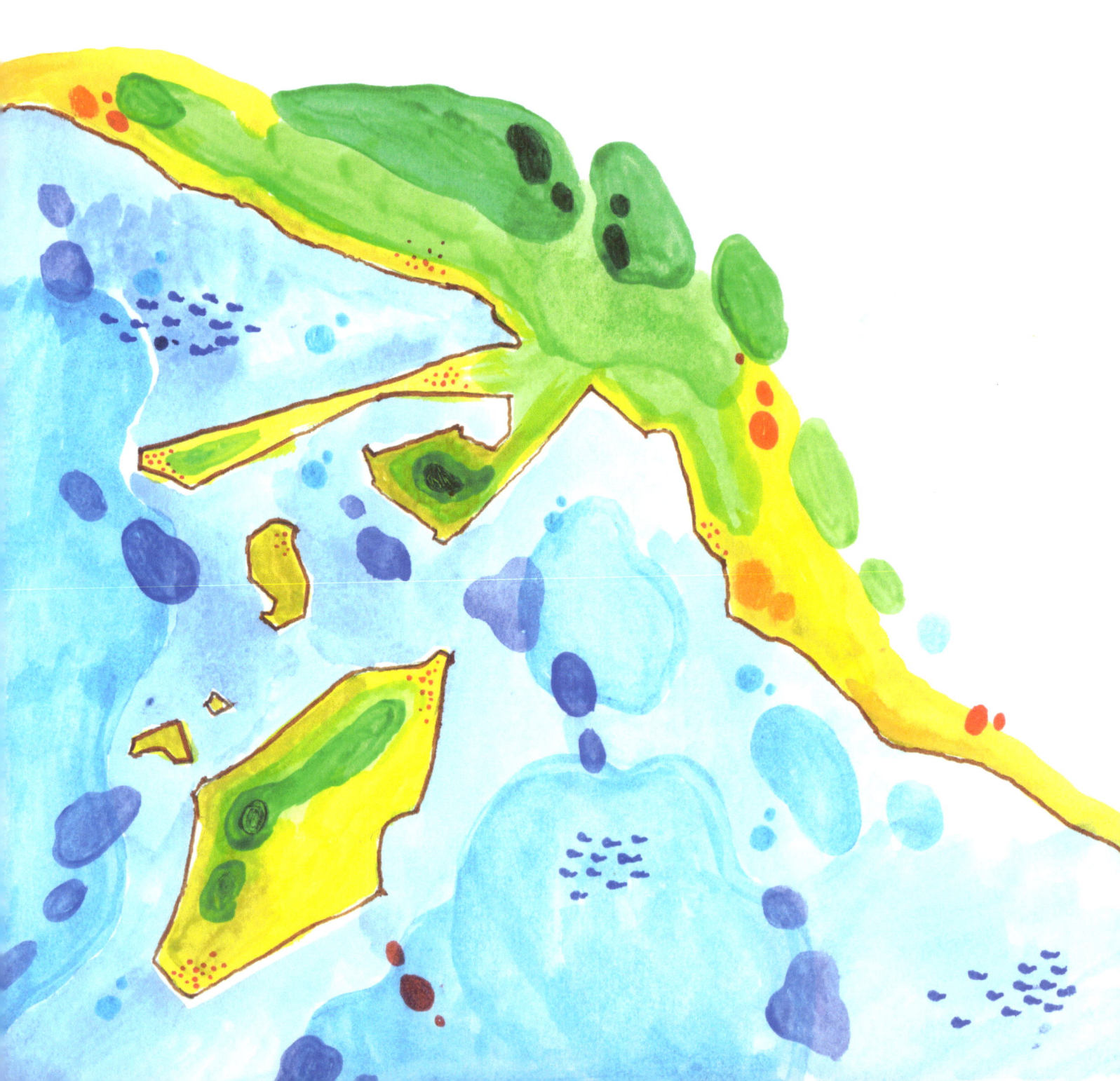

Since he was little, Lonnie has dreamt of becoming a knight and somewhat of a Don Quixote, with armor and a wise horse who will be his best friend and partner. So, he made his own submarine. He wants to travel far and wide and protect the sea and its life.
Every so often Papa Bountiful scolds him:
"Quit daydreaming, Lonnie!" he says.
"But, Papa," says Lonnie. "I intend to be a knight.
I am serious."

And there is another thing: Lonnie is in love.
His mind is constantly on Regina, the herring
from Santa Marina, a little prima ballerina.

He met her a while ago at a party thrown by Mrs. Ida the crayfish from Florida. Since then he can think of nothing else. She danced ballet while he played the clarinet, and her sight made him swoon.

He sends her letters every day with Mr. Swordfish, the mailman, and in them he always encloses a poem, like this one:

Beautiful girl of the sea shores
Eyes like yours
laced in yellow all around
are nowhere else to be found
They bedazzle me and
I want you to learn
that in my sleep, I toss and turn
for you I yearn
and cannot do
away from you

But Regina is such a coquette! She writes to Lonnie she will only love someone daring and adventurous. She notes that the son of the Sea Bream is very polite and every day brings her silky ribbons made of seaweed and vows to do the most extraordinary feats for her.

There is another reason why Lonnie wants
to become a knight:
to win the heart of Regina the herring from Santa Marina.
If he has to, he will duel with the son of the Sea Bream.
So he decides to enroll in knight school and get started on an
adventurous journey to prove his love.
He puts on a shiny armor of seashells
and takes up a long sharp sword.

"Farewell and be careful,"
Mrs. Mina, his mother, says weeping.
"Make sure you love the sea and help the creatures in it. That will
make you a valiant knight and me, a proud lobster," his father, Mr.
Bountiful, advises him.

All by himself Lonnie makes his plans. His small submarine, stocked with maps and supplies, sets out.

On the way the little lobster happens upon Dwight, the seahorse from the Isle of Wight. He is lost in the deep and cries for help.

"I've lost my backpack with all my belongings and all my money in it. What will become of me now?"

Dwight the seahorse whimpers.

"Fear not! I will help you find your way. If we voyage together, we will not get lost," says Lonnie confidently as he spins around once.

"I do love adventures so! But I am scared of mussels and clams. Ooh, the way they open and shut their shells and won't leave me alone..." complains Dwight, sniffling.

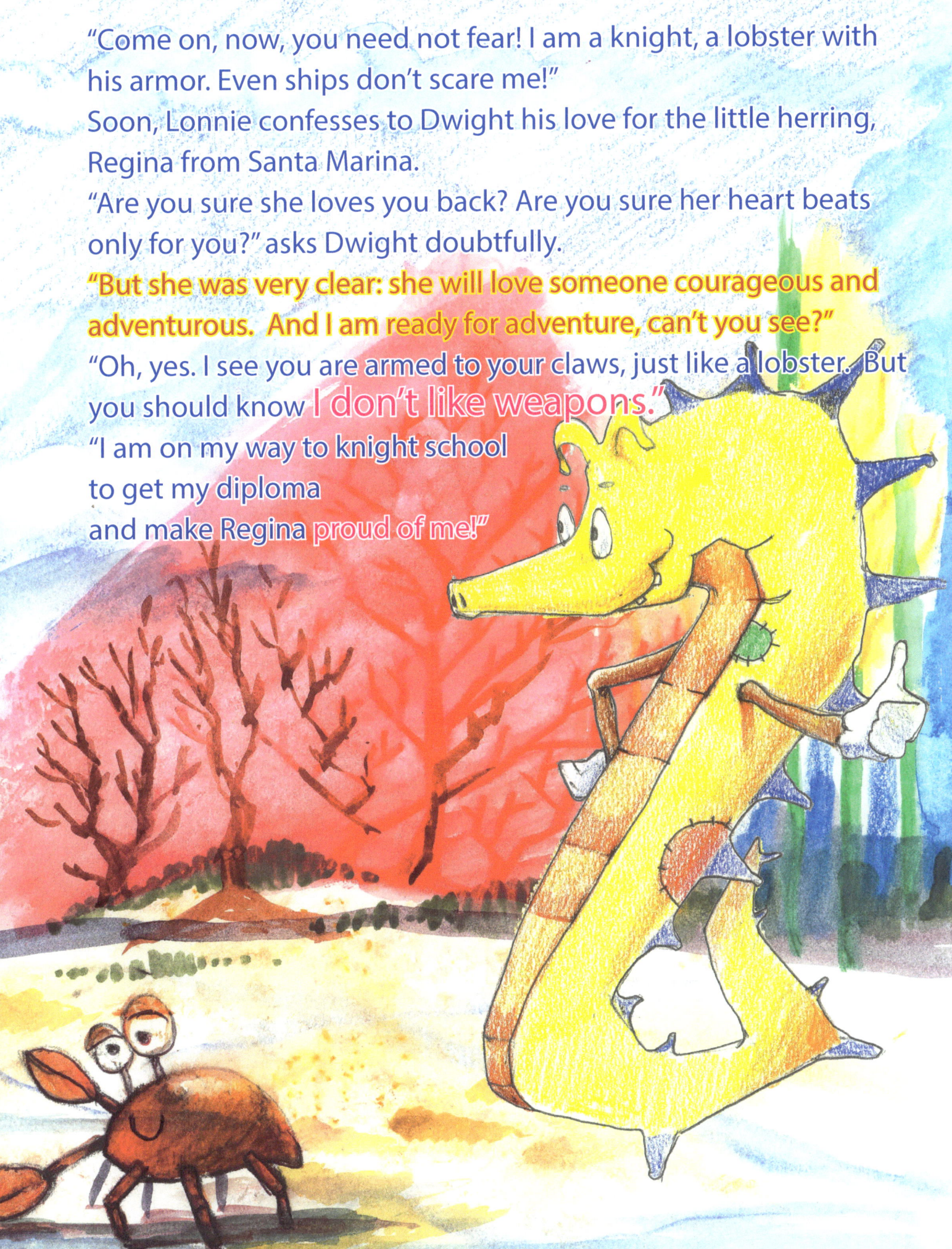

"Come on, now, you need not fear! I am a knight, a lobster with his armor. Even ships don't scare me!"

Soon, Lonnie confesses to Dwight his love for the little herring, Regina from Santa Marina.

"Are you sure she loves you back? Are you sure her heart beats only for you?" asks Dwight doubtfully.

"But she was very clear: she will love someone courageous and adventurous. And I am ready for adventure, can't you see?"

"Oh, yes. I see you are armed to your claws, just like a lobster. But you should know I don't like weapons."

"I am on my way to knight school
to get my diploma
and make Regina proud of me!"

Dwight does not quite understand but he decides to follow Lonnie. He has a feeling that they will be best friends. So, together like the two claws of a lobster, Lonnie and Dwight defy the strong currents and the foamy sea.

Because they can't both fit into the submarine they turn it into a surfboard.

So they put out for the deep waters of knight school, when suddenly they spy ahead a monster with an orange tail.

"Oy, dear mother, I'm scared!" Dwight the seahorse screams and hides in a nearby cave.

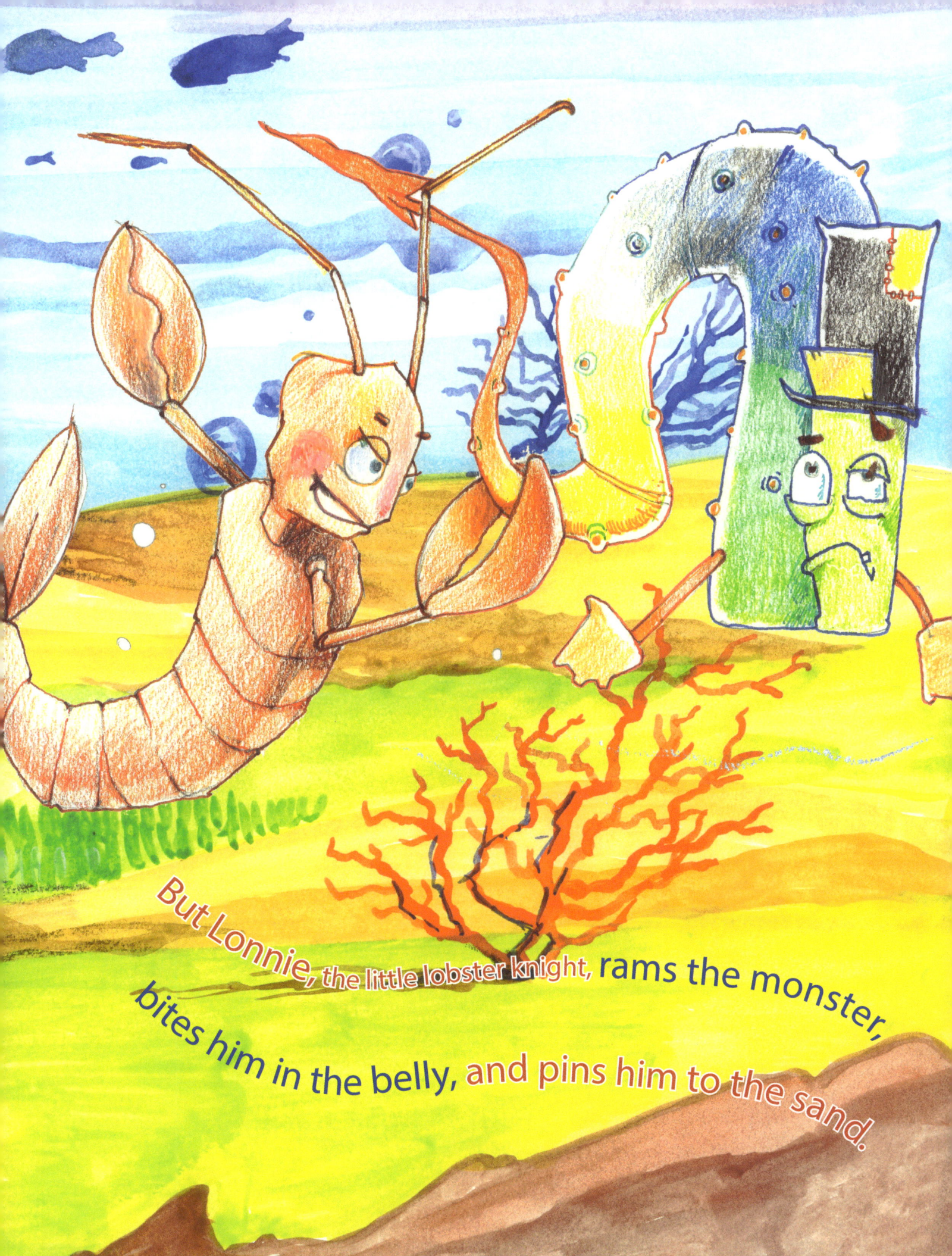

But Lonnie, the little lobster knight, rams the monster, bites him in the belly, and pins him to the sand.

"Why did you pinch me with your sharp claws?" asks the monster.
"Because you are a monster and I am a lobster who will be famous one day," answers Lonnie courageously.

"For the pretty eyes of a herring," adds Dwight shyly and peeks from behind the corals.
"I am a knight and help the creatures of the sea."
"Knight-shmight!"
"Who is Shmight? I am the knight!"
"Well, if you really want to help like the knight you say you are, go to the waters around Ibiza. There little Delphe, the pretty she-dolphin, got caught in a fisherman's net and is struggling to free herself. I am on my way to report on the incident."

"You see, I am the famous reporter Monster Della-te-of the well-known family."

"What? **Della-te-Ras?** I only know **Ras-mass** the Squid-Ogre from the waters of the Riviera," says Lonnie.
"And I know Ban-Te-Ras-Troll a career actor,"
adds Dwight, laughing.
"Come, I will show you the way. If we band together, we can save Delphe," says Della-te-Ras.
So then, packed like sardines in the small submarine, all three reach the waters of Ibiza. They get down to work immediately to save Delphe from the nets. They try for hours but instead they tangle the nets even more.
Then Lonnie lets out a loud cry.

"**Everyone, stand back!**" And holding his sword he rushes forward. He saws through the nets with his claws, cuts them with his sword and... gets himself tangled in them, while **adorable Delphe** glides relieved into her mother's arms.
Everyone is cheering! Other dolphins gather round along with all kinds of fish: bream and snappers, sardines and carp, a tuna and a shield of lobsters. The news spreads quickly and the picture of Lonnie wrapped in the nets makes the round of **the seven seas.**

"Do you suppose Regina has read the papers? Will she be proud of me, I wonder?" Lonnie

"Oh, sure she'll be proud of you when she sees you hanging in the net. What a catch, she will think,"
laughs the monster out loud.
"If she does not want him, Lonnie will take it to heart," Dwight interrupts.
So, the days go by. The three friends wander the seas to get **to knight school**. Lonnie because he wants to help the sea world, Dwight because he wants to help Lonnie, and the monster because he wants to help himself by selling big news to his boss, **Mr. Sea Bass.**

On the way they decide to rest a while at the inn of Mr. Mullet. As they are eating and drinking they hear voices coming from afar.

"Mr. Suction-Cup Three-Heart, the octopus, got trapped inside a trunk in the old shipwreck."

"Let's go!" says Lonnie. "The octopus needs us."
As soon as they arrive at the sunken ship,
Lonnie takes action.
"Stand back, everyone!" he shouts.
"I will open the trunk."
With his sword he breaks the lock, lifts the heavy lid with his claws and frees the octopus.
Everyone is applauding and cheering.
But they have not realized that someone is missing.
Lonnie the lobster, the famous knight, banged against the lid of the trunk and is on his way to the hospital with a big bump on his head.

"Hero saves octopus from trunk in old shipwreck!" read the headlines in **News of the Deep.**

In the picture Lonnie looks miserable with a bump on his head.
"I have made a hero out of you," boasts Della-te-Ras.
"Everyone is talking about you!"
"This is the first time I see a hero with a hump," answers Dwight.

"Bump," the monster corrects him.

"Hump, bump, it's the same thing."

Heroic rescue!

After a week in the hospital of the deep, Lonnie is ready to start classes in knight school. The lessons begin and he does not miss even one. He is first in fencing, first in archery, in horse-riding and in track. His only problem is the food. It includes:

Seaweed. Seaweed tea. Seaweed soup with plankton. Seaweed soufflé. Seaweed salad. Seaweed stew. Seaweed pie. Seaweed biscuits. Seaweed juice. Seaweed with seaweed for something different.

With diploma in hand Lonnie leaves knight school but a big surprise is waiting for him. Suction-cup Three-Heart the octopus, Delphe the dolphin, a shield of lobsters, and of course the carp, Dwight and the monster have prepared an amazing graduation party for him. Lonnie, truly moved, thanks them each and all for their love and promises (a big thing for a knight to promise) that he will always be there for them.

Before too long, Lonnie learns all the rules of knight school by

RULES OF A GOOD KNIGHT

A good knight must be fair

A good knight must face adversity with a smile

A good knight must be courageous

A good knight must eat healthy

A good knight must always be polite (and say "thank you" and "please")

A good knight must be generous

A good knight must help all those in need

A good knight must do nice things for his beloved

A good knight must respect others and the environment

A good knight must be honest and work well with others

A good knight must love peace and freedom

At that very moment, Dela-te-Ras the monster receives an urgent phone call. It is his editor. Mr. Sea-Bass who screams the news:
"Tourists have camped on the beach of Reta, the caretta-caretta, the loggerhead turtle. She and her friends have fled. No-one knows where they are and they cannot lay their eggs now."
"Let's go! I am ready" calls Lonnie in his knight voice.
"Oh, mother seahorse, weep for your son. I do not like weapons!"

"**We don't need weapons**, Dwight. We only need our brains to win this one," says Lonnie.
So they all set out together. It's a long way to their destination.
"Dwight, send word to the other lobsters to come here. We need them. **I have a plan.**"

Breaking news:

"Tourists have camped all over the beach. Caretta-caretta and her friends cannot come out on shore to lay their eggs. **They are in danger.**"

As soon as they arrive, Lonnie prepares the lobsters for battle. It is a strange battle formation. One on top of the other, holding on tight to each other, they form a high wall. They move in this formation and they are a scary sight to behold.

Lonnie is at the front and in full armor. With the air of a knight he gives the sign: **"Ready!"**

The lobsters move on in their formation.
They are enormous.
When they emerge from the sea
and the swimmers and sun-bathers see them
they run screaming: "Monster! Monster!"

They pull out their umbrellas,
grab their beach chairs, and shoving
and pushing leave helter-skelter.
In the prevailing madness,
Lonnie yells: **"Let's go!"**

The bravest of the beach-
goers, covered in sunscreen
and lotion, stand to face
Lonnie and his lobsters. But
they, too, shake in fear at
the sight of this unusual
monster. Lonnie encourages
his troops:
**"Stay close, have no
fear of sun-screen!"**

Shortly the suspense is over. Lonnie and his friends manage to chase the tourists from the beach.
But a strange man still stands there, holding a net in his hand.

"Is there something you want, Mister?"
"Yeah, bud, I feel like lobster today," the man answers with nerve.
"Cut it out. We've had it with all of you and your taste for lobster sauce on your pasta."
Lonnie rushes forward and bites the man with the net. The man turns around running. He is still going.

Dwight runs to his friends joyfully and says:
"You did it, Lonnie! Hurray!"
"We all did it, Dwight. **All of us together!**"
Dela-te-Ras the monster sends his report to Mr. Sea-Bass. His
colleagues spread it all over the world:

"**Reta's beach is only for Reta and her friends, the other
caretta–caretta turtles. No swimming allowed.**"

Reta and the other turtles thank them all for their valuable help.
The rest of the day, Lonnie is interviewed for the papers. The
news reaches Regina who then rushes to him to congratulate
him with kisses and a big hug.

Well, she had said it clearly: she would love
only a daring and adventurous suitor. And
Lonnie dared, not only for Regina but for all
the inhabitants of the sea.

Lonnie almost faints looking at her: her oceanic beauty and grace, her tickly kisses are more than he can bare and he swoons. All shook up he asks her again:

"And the son of the Sea-Bream?"

"Oh, my dear Lonnie, knight of my heart and Don Quixote of my life, I have eyes for no one but you," she says sweetly.

Then Lonnie picks himself up and sings with joy and shining smiles:

"There is no other to be seen
in the deep or in the high seas
more desirable and fine a herring
than the beautiful Regina.
I look at you and sigh
As I am swooning all the while
Sinking deeper and deeper more
until I hit the sea floor.
There I find a sea shell
with lips half-open,
who graciously asks me, "Well,
shall I give to you a pearl?"
"Yes," I say.
He gives it to me
and I surface with a whirl,
I want to give it to you, only you
so you can see how I want you, I do
my beautiful herring, Regina,
and my heart's true ballerina!".

From that day on Lonnie the knight and his Regina are inseparable. He is the knight of the seven seas and she is the prima ballerina in the
Ballet of the Deep.
And Dwight does not feel lonely any more. He is with his best friend and is always willing to help.
Monster Dela-te-Ras has become a one-of-a-kind reporter famous for his coverage of sea-matters.
And they all have given a promise that they will never allow anyone to destroy the sea because it belongs to them, it is their home and it is precious.
If you, too, want to **help** Lonnie the Lobster and his friends, remember every time you are at the sea, he may appear before you, **ready to protect the sea and the beaches.**

The End